BDSM DARK SEX:

8 Unraveled Explicit Stories For Adults

VOL. 2

I would like to invite you to read another one of my books that I think you will really enjoy.
The book is called:

"Filthy Sexy Stories For Adults: 10 Short Exciting and Spicy Stories"

Enjoy!

Table of Contents

WELCOME HOME

Bondage Bdsm Story

You come home from work and find me waiting for you. I am wearing a French maid uniform with white thigh highs and black stiletto heels. I lead you to the bathroom where a robe and toiletries are ready for you. Relaxing music is playing.

"We have about half an hour until dinner is ready, Sir."

You take a long hot shower after your night at work and find your favorite shampoos and soaps waiting for you. You find me in the kitchen preparing dinner. I turn and smile,

"We have a few minutes until dinner if you would like to watch TV. I made you a rum and coke. It is in by the couch."

You smile and lean down to kiss the back of my neck, knowing that it makes my pussy instantly wet.

"What are we having, hun?"

"Grilled steaks, with sautéed mushrooms and onions. Twice baked potatoes and a Mediterranean salad. For dessert strawberry short cake."

I feel your hands brushing up my legs, pulling my skirt up to reveal my black lace boy shorts. I lean back into you and you pull my hair to turn my head, kissing me hard; your tongue chasing mine. I break away from you.

"Sir, if you keep distracting me dinner will be ruined. Please have a drink and relax."

I smile at you.

You leave me in the kitchen and find a tv tray in the living room with the remote and a drink sitting by your favorite chair. A few minutes later I bring in our dinner. We eat and discuss our day while you search the TV for some entertainment. After we have eaten, I take your dishes,

"Sir, if you go lay on the bed it is time for your massage."

You look at me as though you are going to argue, but I am off to the kitchen putting the dishes in the washer and cleaning the kitchen. You walk to the bedroom to find candles lit, fresh sheets on the bed, music playing and oil sitting by the bed. You lie down on your back and start to drift with the music. I come into the room and start with a light massage of your head and face, working down to your arms, and then your legs. I use long slow strokes to relax your body. Then I sit at the end of the bed and use a vanilla lotion to massage your feet.

"Have you ever had your feet rubbed babe?" I ask you softly.

But you can only moan. I help you roll over on to your stomach and work the back of your legs and your back, making sure to stretch out your lower back and sciatic area, running my fingernails lightly across your back. As I finish your massage I lean down and whisper in your ear:

"Anything else you want, Sir?"

You moan 'yes', and before I can react you grab me and pull me down under you, pinning me to the bed. You kiss me and run your hands down my body feeling the satin of the maid outfit. You can feel my lacy bra and your hand runs down my stomach to my lacy panties. You rub my clit and I moan into your mouth as your tongue teases mine. You lean back and smile at me.

"Yes, there is something I want", and you pull out a set of silk ties. "Remember what we talked about this morning?"

I nod yes.

"Tell me what you want," you say to me.

I blush. "I want you to tie me up, shave my pussy, and tease and fuck me until I beg you to stop."

You smile at me and raise my hands above my head tying them to the bed and then move to the end of the bed and tie my legs spread eagle to the bed. You place a pillow under me to raise me up off the bed and lay a towel down and bring warm water, saving cream, and a razor from the bathroom. I am squirming with anticipation. You place your hand on my stomach, right above my hips, to stop my moving. With the other hand you pull the black lacy panties down my legs and pull them over my feet. You spread a thin layer of saving cream over my pussy. I close my eyes and feel your warm hands gliding over my body. A few moments later I feel the razor slowly take the first strip off of my pussy.

"You ok babe?" you ask me.

I nod my head 'yes', unable to speak. You continue to shave me until my pussy is soft and naked. You use the warm water with a washcloth and clean off the remaining shaving cream. The warmth makes me moan. You slip a finger into my pussy and I try to sit up to look at you, but the ties hold me to the bed. You slowly pull your finger out of me while my muscles and hips try to pull you back in. I moan in protest and you lean up to look me in the eye.
"Baby you need to behave or I will blindfold you," you say to me, trying to look stern.

"Yes Sir," I pout.

You stand up and walk out of the room. I start to protest and you give me a look that tells me I really shouldn't. I lay there waiting, listening to the music I turned on for your massage and slowly I relax, forgetting that I am even tied to the bed, naked and under your control. You return to the room with a box, of what I can only assume contains the objects you have been thinking about using on me all day.

"I am going to blindfold you hun, I know you have behaved, but I want you to feel everything." My eyes widen but I don't say anything to you. The wetness on my thighs tells you everything. You place the large black blindfold over my eyes. I feel you slide your hand under me and unzip the maid's uniform and pull from my body. I can feel your eyes running down my body. From my black lacy bra that holds my tits up high, down to my white thigh highs and heels. You put your box of tricks on the bed, so that they are close to us at all times. You untie my arms and I feel you unhook my bra and pull it up my arms, so that I am naked for you. Then you tie my arms again.

I suck in air as I feel an ice cube tracing around my left nipple and then slowly run over to trace my right nipple as well. The cold makes them stand at attention. Your warm tongue flicks over my left nipple as the ice trails slowly around the right. You suck the nipple into your mouth and my back arches towards you.

"Hun, if you misbehave like that again I will have to punish you and I don't want to have to do that." You whisper up to me, returning to work on my tits.

My body is on fire and it is taking everything in me not to move. The ice moves down my chest as your mouth moves on to the right nipple. You bite me slightly, knowing it makes my pussy wet to be bitten. Then, your tongue follows the ice down my body until you place it on my clit.

"Ahhh, God," I can't stop myself from moaning.

You smile knowing how hard it is for me to give up control and how hot and wet it is making me.

You slip the ice cube into my pussy while you lick my clit. My body jerks at the cold of the ice and the heat of your mouth. Your mouth leaves me to place soft kisses around my pussy, but never on my clit which is where my body is begging for you to touch me. Your finger holds the ice inside my pussy while it melts. You can feel my muscles squeezing at the cold ice and at your finger. You move down so that you are between my legs and my soaked pussy is raised and exposed for your every desire. You lick me, from the cool wetness leaking out of me, up to my clit where you suck hard. I lean my head back and moan aloud. You reach into the box taking out one of my vibrators and slowly slide it into my tight, wet pussy. Watching it open up to envelope the toy that is a just a bit smaller than the size of your own throbbing cock.

I have no idea how you are keeping control, as you slowly turn the knob of the vibrator on until is it as high as it goes.

"UUHHH please," I moan.

"Please, what hun? You ask.

"Please fuck my baby?" I beg.

"No hun, I am not done with you yet. I know you can take more than this." You slowly start fucking me with the vibrator. My breathing is getting heavier by the second and your thrusts become quicker and you watch my pussy squeeze tight, trying to hold on to the vibrating cock. I start to whimper and you know I can't take this speed much more. You pull the toy from me, returning it to the box. I am lost in darkness my pussy yearning at the air, longing to find any part of you.

"AGGGHHH fuck!"

I feel hot wax drizzle across my tits. Just as I calm down another drizzle onto my belly. My body quivers. You use one hand to spread my pussy juices down to my ass, while the other hand removes the wax from my body. Each time your finger grazes my asshole my hips buck.

You lean up and remove the blindfold, kissing me deeply and letting me suck on your tongue. My body is on fire and I want you so badly right now. I will let you do anything. You know this. You roll so that you are between my legs as we kiss. I feel your hard cock against my pussy. I sigh softly and you push your cock all the way into my pussy in one hard thrust while you cover my mouth with your own. I moan into your mouth. Your cock is tight in my little pussy and it drives me crazy. My hands are clenched above our heads and my breathing is short and shallow. You lean back so you can look at my face.

Slowly you start shallow thrusting into my pussy, the muscles melting around your cock, molding it to your desire.

"That's it. Let me take you Destiny."

As your thrusts become quicker and more urgent, my

moans become louder. You pull your cock almost all the way out of my pussy and slam it back in. It feels so good that I haven't noticed that you have untied my hands from the headboard and tied them together behind your neck.

"Ahhh, yes fuck me hard, ahhh, please baby," I beg you.

You thrust faster than ever and I can feel your cock growing just a little inside of me. I know you are going to come and I am about to come too. You pull my feet free from the ties, and roll me over onto my stomach. I feel you pull my hips up to you and your cock sinks back into my pussy. From the box of tricks you find my small glass dildo and tease my ass with it slowly pushing it in.

"It's....so....tight....I'm gonna cum...oh...please."

I can feel you balls slapping against my clit and your hand drive the dildo into my ass in time with each thrust of your cock. You slap my ass hard and my muscles contract around your cock and don't loosen up.

"Oh ......fuck.....yes" I scream. Your hot breath is on the

back of my neck.

"Come with me," you yell and slap my ass again.

My pussy oozes all over your balls and you shoot my pussy full of your cum in three more thrusts. We collapse on our sides with you and the dildo still inside of me. My thigh highs are drenched and we cannot move; for a long time we breathe more and more softly.

You finally lean forward and kiss the back of my neck. "Mmm. I should call you sir more often."

I giggle.

BUZZING FEMDOM

Femdom Bdsm Story

John inserted the key into his front door as quietly as he could. He slipped inside, putting his laptop case down ever so gently, and closed his eyes for a moment. Oh, hello you! There she was, padding barefoot down the stairs. She did not come to him; she stopped three steps up, so that her womanly pubis was level with his mouth, so that he had to look up to her, almost look up her. Today she had on a plain black cotton t-shirt and a plain black cotton miniskirt. He knew that under the skirt would be plain white cotton knickers. At the height she stood they were a hair's breadth from being visible to him.

Sandra's soft brown eyes looked at John. The urgent feminine greed he saw there unnerved him now as it did every evening when he returned home. Her lips were parted, her slim body faced his, her face was tilted down and her straight, shoulder length hair swung forward a little. There were no words, but her plea was loud and clear. Come upstairs with me now. Come up and give me what I need. Now. Right now.

In the bedroom Sandra undressed him with practiced and efficient grace. Short-sleeved shirt, tie. With submissive obedience he lifted each foot so she could remove his shoes, socks and trousers. She did not hurry, but he felt her anticipation, her delayed gratification. It had become a ritual of helplessness for him, each step taking away the need for him to participate, each devotional act confirming his passive role. She knelt before him and slowly pulled down his briefs. He was already made hard by the anticipation of his wife's attentions and their inevitable outcome. Now he stood naked and erect. Utterly submissive.

As part of her ceremonial preparation Sandra washed John's genitals. She used a soft flannel soaked in cool water with a dash of lemon-scented bath oil. He knew she had learned to take her time because any sense of pressure or urgency would reduce his output. He knew that from this point and for the next few hours her sole aim was to make him come as many time as he was able, and for each pulsing orgasm to produce as much semen as possible. Their physical relationship had turned from something sexual and mutual into something parasitic. No, not parasitic, because parasites took from their hosts and gave nothing back. This was symbiosis. She took his creamy fluid, all he could manage, and in return she gave him orgasms, through the evening and into the night, leaving him in a state of dizzy, throbbing exhaustion that had become addictive for him.

At first, as he realised what was happening to them, John had tried to turn the ceremony back to what had been before, something more normal. He would reach for her knickers, roll over on top of her, kiss her nipples. But each time, with beautiful, gentle authority, she guided him back to her path, led him to her needs. And, oh, how he would succumb. Succumb. It was the perfect word for what he did. He was sucked; he would come. She would suck, until he came again. Suck. Come. Suck. Come.

When he asked her why, she told him it was what she wanted. When he wondered if it was what he wanted his throbbing, aching member betrayed him, playing stupid, helpless slave to the mastery of her cunning lips. A masculine glimmer of rebellion flashed through him, as it often did at this stage, just before the relentless sucking started. He had the impulse to kneel down, pull her up to her feet, hold her, kiss her, undress her, fuck with her. With. Together. But she always seemed to sense this moment and her soothing, teasing massage would slow and intensify, stroking away his impulse and his will.

His role was to be sucked. At this moment it was what he wanted too. As he relaxed he could feel his cock harden even more, and his moment of uncertainty would melt away under Sandra's cool, wet rubbing and his own surging need for release. He lay back on the bed with his breath catching in his throat. She tied his wrists to the bedhead. She had learned that this excited him, increased his capacity. She lay down next to him smiling and looked lovingly at him. Was it love? He let this final flit of worry dance into the shadows and closed his eyes. He was strong and fit, but he needed to save all his athletic prowess for what was to come. He felt her hair brush lightly but deliciously over his thighs. Her delicate fingers closed around his bulging cock and began to slide his foreskin back and forth in slow, gentle strokes.

In the six months since the sucking had first started John had gone through several stages of wonder and disbelief at how good Sandra had become at doing the things she did to him. All his previous experience of being masturbated by a woman, including her, was a mix of pain and dissatisfaction. They would push down too hard on his foreskin, hold his cock too low down, go too fast, squeeze too hard, keep changing hands. The worst times were when they stopped stroking, as if caught by surprise at his ejaculation.

But driven by her need to express and taste his fluid, Sandra had learned well. Her fingers curled around his cock an inch from his tip, sliding his foreskin slowly back and forth over the helmet of his penis. She did not push it down all the way, her strokes were just long enough to stretch his sliding skin over the base of his helmet and then back up almost, but not quite, to his tip. She started with thumb and forefinger curled around his hot shaft, a gentle but insistent rhythm, two or three strokes a second.

He knew she would not stop or vary this perfect, delicious motion until she made him come. The certainty of her relentless stroking allowed him to slip into semi-consciousness. As he surrendered carelessly into erotic catatonia his breathing slowed. The bed bounced softly as her hand worked its up and down magic on his rock hard shaft. He was getting close now, his breaths deepening, and he felt that lovely, involuntary physical sensation of fluid flowing in his balls, moving, filling tubes and pipes, waiting to explode out of his body and into her sweet, sweet mouth. He felt her lips close gently around his tip and, without disturbing the slow, pistoning rhythm of her hand, they began to suck him. He knew that she spent a lot of her day at home working out, strengthening her muscles and her breathing while she waited eagerly for his return.

Each time now it felt that her sucking was becoming more intense. Tonight it was almost too much and he gasped as he felt the force of her oral suction on the end of his cock, as if she was going to suck him inside out. Her hot saliva lubricated his throbbing tip, ensuring a perfect suction seal that was so strong he could feel the end of his penis expand inside her mouth and sense the blood being pulled into his shaft making it even harder and longer. It was erotically primitive, this sense of something, someone, her, her mouth, wanting, needing, demanding, sucking, feeding, pulling, drawing his fluids out of him and into her. Her tongue caressed his bulging helmet inside her hot, wet mouth and he succumbed. Completely. Oh, fuck. Oh, fuck. Thick, hot gouts, spurting, squirting deep into her, trying to fulfil, trying to sate. Great pulses of pleasure coursed through his loins, surging more and more of his creaminess up his throbbing shaft and discharging it over her honey sweet tongue, into her eager, swallowing throat. He came and came, gave her everything he had. Oh, fuck. Oh, fuck! When will it stop?

He was panting, sucking in great gulps of air. His head was spinning and his vision sparkled as the world seemed to tip and sway with the shuddering intensity of his endless climax. As his euphoric insanity cleared he sensed her final savouring and swallowing of him, heard her sigh, felt her lips open and move down his still pulsing cock, sucking and licking, slowly and firmly, making sure they did not lose a single drop. She too was breathing hard, giving little shivers of delight against him. It felt like a deeper need, beyond sex. He didn't want to understand it. Perhaps she didn't either. But she indulged herself in that need, submerged herself in it totally, and she was pulling him in with her.

Sandra left John for a few minutes. When she came back she had a glass of orange juice and a bowl of yoghurt. She did not untie his hands. Instead she help the glass to his lips and then fed him with a spoon. He drank and ate everything. It reinforced his obedient submission. It occurred to him that apart from her greeting when he had arrived from work, the only words uttered between them were his vocal ejaculations as he came. He opened his mouth, as if to attempt conversation. Several times he had wanted to ask if she put something in the drink, something that helped him come so many times. But this too now seemed unimportant. What mattered was how many times. He swallowed his final mouthful and she leaned forward to kissed his lips, leaving a wasteful glaze of his semen on them. Her big brown eyes looked into his and he gave her what she was seeking, total acceptance of her need, total surrender to her ordeal by oral sex. Yes, he was ready for her.

Without a word she climbed over him and faced down the bed so that her knees were either side of his head, resting against his shoulders. He looked up her short skirt at her white knickers. They were a few inches from his mouth. He wanted to reach up and kiss them but his hands were tied and he knew he had to remain still and passive. Only when she sensed his complete calm would she open her knees and let her hot gusset press against his mouth. It was another discovery, his powerful sexual response to being smothered by her panties. Through weeks of learning they had found that simple, white cotton worked best. Simple white cotton always made him come again. Her hot, cotton covered sex pressed against his open mouth and his nose. He had to strain to breathe and each struggling inhalation drew into him the sense and the spicy smell of her gently squirming vagina. His questing, tasting tongue rasped against the hot dryness of the fabric, moistening, oiling, so he could better feel the outline of her vulva as it rocked across his mouth.

He was helplessly erect. Again he felt her hair brush against his thighs and again he gasped as her mouth slid slowly over his helmet enclosing it in her wet, irresistible vacuum which only he could fill. Her hand was already pumping his hard shaft, gliding up and down with exquisite relentlessness. He opened his legs and, at this invitation, she moved her other hand which now clasped his testicles and began a gentle, pulsing squeezing. It was an erotically merciless interrogation that always produced his liquid confession; the only question was when.

Now. Oh. Now. I confess. And it hurts, it hurts. His loins thrust up towards her as his fluid jetted into her mouth once more. His aching muscles spasmed with waves of joy and release. His cries of agonised fulfilment were muffled under her genital gag. He strained to take huge, smothered intakes of breath that were laden with the hot smell of her sex. He was blacking out as the final, desperate gouts of his semen left him for her. The cocktail surge of depleted oxygen, ecstasy and pain drained him of his feeling of self. Who was he? He didn't care. He didn't even know.

Slowly he recovered. Hormones of arousal bubbled in his blood and the euphoria of such intense release simplified his reality. He was to be sucked. He wanted to be sucked. She must suck him again. Now she took her panties off and, with the same waiting for his breathing to slow, the same patience, she lowered herself onto his mouth again. A third arousal so soon after orgasm might be painful which is why she kept the lubricant in the fridge. He felt soothing coldness squirt over his hot, throbbing penis. Eased by the cool, slippery jelly, her hand moved differently, sliding up and down the full length of his exhausted cock. The intense taste of her womanhood sliding over his mouth together with the inevitability of her interrogating hands forced his response. He hardened slowly, but she knew how to rebuild his resolution. Cold jelly squirted against him again. It was so soothing and lovely, allowing her hand to move up and down faster and faster, making her body bounce and thrust against his mouth. His tongue twirled inside her, tasting her juices as she too became aroused. Now he needed to sense her excitement in order to give her the answer she needed. Now she started to come, great sobbing cries of joy as his tongue licked and curled against her pulsing, shivering clitoris.

Afterwards, if he remembered, he might wonder how she had become so multi-orgasmic, for this was new as well. In the old days she would lose interest after the first one. Now she was insatiable. Or had she learned that this was the best way to make him produce another orgasm so quickly? Was she faking it just to get what she needed from him? But increasingly he did not remember or wonder. Increasingly she was reducing him to a state of emptied fulfilment that left no desire or space for thought.

Her wet, thrusting vagina smothered him, filling him with another divine cocktail of panic and arousal. Again he felt her lips close over him. Again he felt her suck, harder still this time, the vacuum so strong he could feel it forcing the fluid out of his balls. Again he climaxed, her lips clamped round him and accepting his gouting discharge into her mouth as if she was part of his cock, as if her whole being was a sucking, swallowing extension of his sexuality. Now it felt right, the inevitability of her need and what it meant to them, to him. Now he felt himself being immersed in her obsession, floating away in it, carried by her along a river of orgasmic oblivion that had no end.

Sandra left John a little longer this time. When she returned she had her iPod and some electric toys that she would use on him to ensure his complete emptying. She slipped the headphones onto him and saw a new look in his eyes. There was wonder. There was love mixed with confusion. He felt as if she was gradually sucking him away, swallowing his masculinity, his very meaning. He looked at her beautiful mouth. Her lips were full and soft, inviting him to come inside. Again and again. To perform his role. To be sucked. To feed her mouth with his body. His cock jerked upright as if woken from a dream, as if it was disconnected from him; leaving him so it could spend the rest of its life inside her warm, nurturing mouth, carrying out its own selfish purpose of taking his ever diminishing essence and delivering it into her hot, sucking desire. He felt a final surge of fear, as of a man who realises he is becoming insane, just before the madness steals him away.

There, there. She kissed him lightly on the lips. Her reassurance was wordless. Don't worry. I won't hurt you; I only want one thing from you. That's all I want.

And it's all you want too. Shhh. The stroking and buzzing and sucking went on for hours. At some point deep in the night he whispered hoarsely that he could not come any more. But, as they always did, her clever lips found a way, sucked a little harder. Until he was gone.

SABRINA WILL

Spanking Bdsm Story

Fresh out of college I took a job at a marketing firm on Madison Avenue, making terrible wages and working for a terrible boss. Her name was Sabrina Sexton, and for a while I thought she was actually insane.

It wasn't that she worked us hard, if you're young and ambitious enough to go to NYC for a job you expect to be worked hard. Instead, at times she seemed schizophrenic. She'd heap praise on me in the morning and the scream at me in the afternoon. She'd tell me what she wanted, and after I had followed her instructions to the letter, she'd threaten to fire me for wasting the company's time on bullshit.

Of course employees talk, and we certainly talked about her. When I speculated she was literally crazy, someone else suggested she had a problem with amphetamines. In all cases we weren't sure how she managed to first get her job, and then keep it.

Some of us expected she must have slept with the big boss. Sabrina was smoking hot, even for a woman 15 years older than me. Single and no kids so she spent a good deal of her free time at the gym. At least, when she talked about off time, that's what she talked about.

She was average height, about 5'5" with a fit body that had just the right slope from her waist to her hips. Her hair was chestnut brown, but it was difficult to tell how long it was because she always wore it up revealing an elegant neck. Her glasses gave her a bit of that sexy librarian vibe.

Still despite being meticulously put together, she seemed a mess. She had talent for the marketing world, there was no doubt about that, but she was not a leader. We succeeded as a team in spite of her.

One day, in the middle of a preparing for a big client presentation, I had had computer troubles and the IT guys had screwed around and robbed me of a few hours of my life. So when everyone else was leaving for home, I was stuck finishing my end of the product.

My friend Charlie, a well-manicured Latino who I'm pretty sure was gay patted me on the back and smiled, "You sure you want to be alone here with the bitch?

Who knows what she'll do with only one person to scream at." Sabrina was still in her office, a glass encased box on one side of the room, but she kept the blinds drawn.

I laughed and said, "I'm gonna have to brave it, Charlie. If you don't see me tomorrow tell my parents I love them." He laughed as he made his way to the elevator.

Sure enough about 20 minutes later, Sabrina's door opened and she looked around the office, confused at its emptiness. When her eyes fixed on me, they narrowed and she barked, "You. Get in here. Now."

"Great," I thought to myself, "Thanks IT." But I dutifully made my way toward her office and walked in.

"Close the door," she ordered. When I started to say there was no need since we were alone she cut me off and through gritted teeth she said, "A simple goddamn order and you can't even do that without 50 fucking complaints."

I rolled my eyes to myself as I shut the door. Trying to maintain a pleasant disposition in order to end this meeting quickly I said, "So Ms. Sexton, what can I do for you?"

"For starters you can redo all of the copy on the recent campaign," she said tossing a file of paper work at me.

"Um," I started taken aback, "I'm a graphic artist, not a copy writer."

"So you don't know how to write fucking English?" She insulted me. "You went to college, didn't you? Surely your degree made you take writing classes."

I didn't really know what to say, "Well, I could try, but I still have to finish the graphics we decided on, and that will take me a while."

"Jesus Christ," she muttered, "Useless, all of you are fucking useless."

It was the end of a long day so I said the first thing that came to mind, "So why don't you just do it yourself then?" It was part frustration, part serious suggestion. I mean, what did she do all day?

She looked a little stunned. "You know what," she said, "Just go home, and don't bother coming back tomorrow."

I shouted, "Are you fucking kidding me?" I needed this job, but I wasn't about to beg for it. "You know what Sabrina, you don't fucking deserve me or anyone else who works in this office."

Her eyes went wide and then narrowed in anger, but I continued, "If you look good to the big boss it's only because people like me work hard despite your so-called leadership. You soak up the praise and the paycheck, but don't deserve shit. You're like a spoiled child and you should be treated like one."

She laughed at me and mocked, "What does that mean? Are you going to spank me?"

The frustration with her and this job took over as I stepped to her, my 6'0 frame dwarfing her own. I all but snarled, "Someone should."

"Like you're man enough," she said sarcastically, but there was a kind of wide-eyed hunger inspired by my aggression. I took her roughly by the back of the neck and pushed her forward over her desk. She whimpered at the rough treatment as I made her bend at the waist.

"What do you think you're doing?" She breathed

huskily. The grey pencil skirt she was wearing accentuated her round ass as her torso rested against her desk. I made no attempt to hold her down as I reached to undo my belt, and she, surprisingly, made no effort to move.

"Sabrina," I said, "I think you've needed someone to put you in your place for a long time, it might as well be me." And I brought my belt down on her still clothed ass.

It wasn't the first time I'd spanked a woman. A girlfriend in college loved it, but I was never truly disciplining her for bad behavior. This was different, my boss needed to learn a lesson.

When the belt smacked against her ass, Sabrina didn't cry out in anger so much as moan a "fuck you, you son of a bitch." I looked at her bent across the desk and her eyes were fixed on me through her glasses. I brought down the belt again, harder this time. She sucked in air through her teeth and then glared at me through the sensation.

"I'm not sure this belt is getting through to you, Sabrina," I said calmly. "Stand up and remove your skirt so I can give you a proper lesson."

She stood in front me, lowered her eyes and bit her lip. She undid the button on her skirt and the zipper. sliding it down her lean, bare legs past her heels, she stepped out of it. Under her skirt was a red lace thong.

"Remove everything, Sabrina," I continued, taking in the site of her half naked body. "Blouse, bra, and thong too."

"Fuck you," she said, but immediately began unbuttoning her shirt, chin to her chest, she watched me closely over the top of her glasses as her fingers worked the buttons. When she slid it off, stood there in just her bra, panties and high heels, I had to swallow hard, but I was determined to keep my role as dominant.
I gave her a steely glance. "Everything."

She hesitated and then reached behind her back undoing her bra. Her breasts were gorgeous, soft milk- white globes about the perfect size for my hands, with pink, erect nipples just waiting to be tweaked and twisted.

I kept myself from reaching out too eagerly, allowing

her to finish her task. She slid her thong down her legs and revealed that she kept herself all but hairless, a thin strip of fine dark hair atop her now exposed cunt.

She went to remove her 4 inch heels, but I stopped her. "No," I said, "those stay on." She immediately stopped what she was doing and waited for a word from me.

Standing there, arms at her sides, head slightly bowed. Wearing nothing but her glasses and her heels, accentuated with what I now saw as the sluttiest shade of red lipstick and fingernail polish, and an almost out of place string of pearls around her neck, giving her an air of dignity at odds with her present position.

I took her by her delicate shoulders and pushed her down over her desk. She caught herself and rested her upper body on her forearms, her naked ass presented high in the air, aided by her heels.

I stepped behind her, put my foot between hers and pushed her legs apart. For the first time I could see how wet she was and I couldn't help but touch her. I pressed my palm against her sex and ground its flat surface against her cunt, feeling my hand slicken with her ample juices.

Sabrina moaned and gyrated her hips. This made me chuckle slightly as I watched her wanton transformation to bitch in heat from just plain bitch. "Jesus Sabrina, you're quite the submissive slut under all that show of authority, aren't you?"

She simply moaned in reply, which inspired me to remove my hand from her cunt and leave her wantonly pushing back against emptiness. I brought the belt down hard on the now bare flesh of her ass. "Answer me, slut."

She whined from the dual stings of pain and humiliation. "I..." she hesitated, "I... don't know."

I brought the belt down hard again and the sharp sound of smacked flesh sounded in the air, followed shortly by her cry.

"You don't know if you're a submissive slut?" I taunted. "You certainly look like a submissive slut from where I'm standing."

Two more quick slaps with the leather from my belt

and she fell forward on the desk, her arms giving way and her cheek pressed flat against the top. She reached one hand behind her, whether in an effort to shield her ass or soothe it, I didn't know, but I wasn't having any of it.

"Oh no, slut," I said. "Your ass is to remain exposed to me as long as I want it to be, and you will take whatever punishment I say you deserve for abusing your employees."

"No," she whimpered, "no, I'll be good." Her eyes were shut and completely unprompted she whispered, "I'll be your good girl."

"You're right, you will be." I grabbed her slender wrist and pulled it away from her reddening ass. Walking to the front of the desk, I removed my silk tie, held her wrists together in one of my hands and wrapped the tie around them, binding her wrists together above her head. She offered little resistance, as I finished the knot. It seemed that part of her wanted to stop this, but some other part, some deeper part wanted, or needed me to continue.

With her hands bound I was free to return working over the soft flesh of her ass which I did, repeatedly bringing my belt down as a stern punishment for her poor management of me and my colleagues.

Reddening the white skin as her howls filled the air. I could see the marks from the strap of my belt crisscross her delicate flesh.

I paused, panting, as she lay writhing across the desk, moaning almost inconsolably.
"Please..." she whimpered, "Please, I'm so close..."

I was dumb struck by her comment, but I noticed for the first times her thighs were damp with the overflow of her cunt. Intrigued as if I could get her to orgasm with the belt I smacked her again, harder this time and she shook violently as she cried out into the room. Again, the belt came down, this time focused to graze her pussy lips which she increasingly exposed and presented to my discipline.

This was enough to send her over as her body violently began to shake and she called out amid the non verbal shrieks, "Oh my god... that's it... oh god you bastard... I'm going to..." At that point I smacked her as hard as I had, and she finished her sentence by screaming

"Cuuuuuuummmmmmm."

I watched in awe as my submissive slut of a boss melted into a pool of pleasure and pain as her body shook violently into orgasm from the mere fact of a spanking. Her face was agony and ecstasy, tears smeared the mascara from her closed eyes while her ruby red lips hung open gasping for air and crying out her divine anguish.

I sat back in her chair, leaving her splayed in front of me a heaving pile of broken and satisfied flesh. My cock was hard, of course, at the display, but fucking her exposed cunt seemed almost anticlimactic compared to the show I had just witnessed inspired by a whipping.

I stared at her body. From my angle I could see her spread legs leading up to her red ass and still quivering cunt. But I could also see her torso across the desk. Her breast smashed against the cold wood and her face with tear stained cheeks and panting mouth.

I stepped behind her and unzipped my pants,
releasing my already hard cock. I kicked her legs

apart, opening her wet pussy, took my cock in my hand and ran the head up and down her exposed slit.

"You're good at telling people what to do, Sabrina," I mocked, "So why don't you tell me to fuck you."

She whimpered but otherwise remained silent. I brought the belt, still in my hand, down hard on her ass. Her legs quaked and a cry filled the room.

"You're not being a very good boss, Sabrina," I said, "You have a willing employee, but you're not making full use of his talents."

She mumbled something I couldn't hear, her whisper a combination of desire and exhaustion. I smacked her with the belt again. "Speak up, slut."

Tears filled her eyes, her face strained to get through the sting, but I could feel her cunt lips quiver and moisten. Dutifully she said, "Please fuck me."

I continued to wet the head of my cock just inside the lips of her cunt. "You can do better than that." I said, and I smacked her ass again.

"Fuck, fuck, fuck," she babbled, "please, fuck me, take me cunt, please just shove it inside me, I'll be a good girl."

With that I pressed into her, shoving my already aching cock into the tight folds of her wet flesh. She was tighter than expected, whether by nature or abstinence, I couldn't say, but she reacted as though she had been branded, lifting her head and arching her back, almost howling as I drove myself home. Pressed deep inside her, every inch of my thick cock was gripped by her flesh. I held myself there, wanting to revel in the feeling of it. I couldn't resist the idea of leaning forward and taking a firm hold of her hair, which had fallen out of its tie. Wrapping my hand in it I pulled back, making her arch her back even more. Holding her hair like a bridle with one hand, I brought the belt down on her ass with the other, as though I was a jockey whipping his mount.

She cried out again and I felt her inner muscles contract around my cock. The feeling was so divine I whipped her again, keeping firm hold of her hair. Her cries filled the room. Only then did I begin to fuck her in earnest, sliding out and pressing hard back into her, each thrust slow and deliberate and deep.

Occasionally I would bring the belt down again and she would sing out in that wonderful mix of pleasure and pain that would accompany a tension in her body that milked my ever invading cock.

Her vocals, became and incoherent mixture of pleas and commands. "Fuck me, yes, harder, harder, please, whatever you want, hurts so good, hurt me, fuck me, use me."

My own timing was getting better. And finally I brought the belt down hard on her backside, causing her to tighten just before I pressed into her, making my thrust rougher and more invasive. And this treatment proved to be all she needed as her body spasmed and collapsed into another orgasm as she all but screamed, "Fuuucckkkk Hurts so good!!"

I was pressing myself to the limit, but I had plans for this abusive slut. As she still shuddered from her orgasm, I pulled out, leaving her cunt obscenely fucking back against thin air. I pulled her by her hair to her feet, spun her toward me and then pushed her down to her knees.

Still holding her hair, she was panting with unfocused eyes as she looked up at me. Her makeup had smeared and her mouth hung open, and I took the opportunity to push my cock into it. Her eyes shot wide at first, but then closed as she sucked my cock as though it were a pacifier.

Her ordeal had left her exhausted, so it was up to me to control the action. I used both hands to hold her head as I proceeded to fuck her mouth. Her moans vibrated through me as I could feel my cock swell against her tongue.

Finally I pulled out, letting my cock erupt onto her face. The first spurt splashed across her nose and glasses, the second more directly on her lips. I shoved back into her mouth for the remaining amount. Whether happy to be used or just oblivious, she sucked and swallowed the rest.

I fell back into her desk chair as I released her, my own legs giving out. She fell back on her haunches, resting against the drawers of her oak desk. Cum covered her face and dripped down to her breasts.

She looked past me with a vacant, satisfied expression.

I reached forward and ran a finger over a glob of cum on her cheek and shoved it into her mouth. Without thinking, she sucked my finger clean.

"Good girl, Sabrina," I said as I fed her my cum from my finger, "Now get to work rewriting that copy. I'm going home."

ISLAND OF SUBMISSION

Submission Bdsm Story

Safely hidden -- or so she imagined -- behind the gardener's shed in a quiet corner of the school grounds Kerry leisurely exhales the smoke from a surreptitious cigarette. Final exams finished there's no harm in kicking back and relaxing. She's taken great pains to avoid detection, doesn't want to blot her academic record and jeopardise a promised university place.

An unexpected hand on her shoulder makes Kerry yelp in fright, turning quickly to discover who has tracked her down. Could be worse, is Kerry's first thought. Rather than a teacher, Kieran, the rather dishy assistant groundsman looms over her. Kerry is far from the only female sixth former to appreciate his saturnine good looks.

"You scared me," gasps Kerry, hurriedly grinding the incriminating evidence under foot.

"Bit pointless," observes Kieran, "you've been caught young lady. We'd better go inside and have a little chat."

Kerry feels a stab of anxiety; he surely isn't intending to report this transgression? With considerable trepidation she follows the dark haired young man into the gloomy confines of his workplace.

"You're not going to..." Kerry lets the sentence hang unfinished, doing her best to project an impression of wide-eyed innocence.

"Tell on you to the teachers, should do by rights," responds Kieran laconically.

"I'm 18, legally old enough to smoke," ventures Kerry with hint of defiance.

"Old enough for a lot of things, but still against school rules. You should know being one of the clever ones in the top set."

"How could you possibly be aware of that?" Kerry is shocked.

"By listening, working on the flowerbeds outside the classroom windows I hear all sorts -- quite enough to know how much trouble you could be in."

"So you'll let me off," whispers Kerry beguiling.

"Never said so," replies Kieran brusquely. "I might choose not to inform the headteacher, but you still deserve to be punished -- smoking's a filthy habit, it's not as if your generation aren't educated about the dangers."

"You're right," Kerry looks downcast, "but what do you mean, punished?"

"Properly, physically, not just for what you've done, as a future deterrent."

"What, like spank me or something? You can't be serious, no one does that anymore."

"Don't seem like you've much of a choice," says Kieran coolly -- think of the consequences if you don't agree."

Kerry does, shuddering at the prospect of her parent's reaction -- "not angry, just very disappointed," followed by weeks of passive aggressive guilt tripping. She can't stand it, better to get this over with.

"Alright", she agrees cautiously, "but you promise not to ever let on?"

"I'll keep my word so long as you do what you're told," he answers firmly, "start by bending over that workbench."

Hesitantly Kerry leans forward, staring fixedly ahead, weight supported on her forearms. Glossy, shoulder-length fair hair partly obscuring her pretty face, uniform blouse tight against straining breasts, skirt - far shorter than regulation length - revealing taught thighs and long straight legs; an altogether enticing prospect.

"Like this?" she enquires timidly.

"Perfect," replies Kieran rolling up his sleeves to reveal tanned forearms, "now get that skirt up girl."

"No, you mustn't make me..."

"You agreed to comply," his tone is so compelling the reluctant girl's fingers scramble to obey, revealing an absolute peach of a bottom covered by dark tights and tiny white knickers.

Kieran experiences an immediate stiffening of his manhood and momentarily can't trust himself to speak, instead placing a restraining hand on of Kerry's slender waist he brings the other sharply down across those deliciously pert nether cheeks.

"OOF!" Kerry grits her teeth, scared to cry out lest someone hear and investigate. Further spanks follow, his work-calloused palm rhythmically slapping her buttocks. Kerry's feet stamp in mute protest as her poor bottom begins to smart and sting.

He stops. She gives an audible sigh. Is that it? Wasn't too bad, bum's smarting yet Kerry is also aware of a rather more enjoyable sensation burgeoning between her thighs.

"That was just the warm-up," asserts Kieran, "we'll have these down," he tugs at the tights and knickers, "and you'll take the rest on the bare."

"The rest! I thought..."

"Don't care what you thought. Time I've finished that bottom's going to be so sore you'll never look at a cigarette again."

Kieran's hard hand applied to bare flesh takes the hurt to a whole new level. Kerry struggles futilely as her delightful derriere burns hotter, yelping and protesting
-- no chance of her staying quiet now - at each subsequent slap.

Another interlude, Kerry looks reproachfully over her shoulder, eyes wet and arse glowing red. Confused by being simultaneously sore and sexually aroused, can he see how wet she is?

Of course Kieran can, and plans to do something about it, just soon as he's concluded Kerry's chastisement in the traditional manner.

"Six of the best should finish you off nicely," he states, ominously swishing a thin, whippy cane through the air. "Pulled these from the rose beds, not really long enough but needs must." Kerry groans in dismay, no point in pleading, she's little choice but to submit.

"Hold the edge of the bench and push your bottom up," he commands.

She obeys but Kieran's not yet satisfied. "Higher," he says sharply. Screwing her eyes tight shut to avoid seeing the scary bamboo Kerry goes up onto her toes and somehow manages to force her posterior further into the air.

It takes all of the young man's self restraint not to fuck her there and then. Instead Kieran delivers the promised half dozen cane cuts to her already well-smacked bottom. Mild in comparison with some he's applied to willing spankees in the past, Kerry is -- for now -- a novice and this caning primarily to ensure her complete compliance with what will follow...

"Done and dusted," he observes as the cane clatters to the floor. Strong hands grasp her hips and Kieran stoops to kiss each brightly burning orb. "You done good girl, turned you on didn't it?'

Blushing in excitement and humiliation Kerry is lost for words. Right then her blouse buttons pop open, giving up the struggle to contain her boobs His hands move to free them from her bra, deliciously teasing hard nipples. Face flushed with pent-up desire, Kerry makes no protest,

"Reckon you need a thorough seeing to young lady," says Kieran loosening his belt. Kerry risks another glimpse over her shoulder just in time to see an impressively erect cock spring from his jeans. Christ, she'll never to be able to fit all that in! Kieran's fingers slide between her juice-slicked labia, thumb circling her pulsing clit.

"Reckon you can take this?" queries Kieran, correctly interpreting her thoughts; a condom wrapper flutters to the ground.

"I'll try," Kerry nervously pushes her hot little tush back towards her erstwhile tormentor, "I'm not a virgin," she adds quickly. Up to a point, her besotted boyfriend usually fumbles the foreplay then comes far too quickly, leaving Kerry frustrated and forced to compete the job herself.

"Good girl," grunts the groundsman, easing the tip of his cock into her velvety slot.

"OMG!" she exclaims in delight as he slowly slides it in, gently stretching her deliciously tight pussy until she's accommodated the full length and girth. He pauses to let Kelly adjust to it filling her sex, lividly marked arse pressing hard against his washboard abdomen. Begins to thrust unhurriedly back and forth, squeezing her tits, carefully upping the pace.

Oh my, the sensation is incredible, like nothing Kerry has felt before. Better even than when fingering herself while indulging a favourite submissive fantasy - the reality of which far exceeds her dreams.

"You're a bad girl," gasps Kieran, in thrall to desire and screwing her faster now, clasping her tenderised bottom cheeks and unleashing a surge of sexual sensation within Kerry's trembling body. Is she a bad girl? Kerry wonders distractedly, if this is what happens to them she'd like to be.

"Oh yes," she yells exultantly. Kieran feels her entire body spasm, his cock gripped clenched tight in her pulsating pussy as Kerry reaches a crescendo and convulsively comes.

Both breathing heavily they take a moment to recover then, with him still rock hard inside, the young woman lasciviously wriggles her hips. Brimming with lust and the vigour of youth Kelly's already good to go again. It's Kieran's turn to feel his arousal surge out of control, pushing hard and deep into her lithe body his own climax fast approaching.

"Oh God yes, go on you bastard, fuck my pussy," screams Kerry, astonished at her industrial language and loss of control. She feels his prick pump inside her, dimly hears an animal growl of satisfaction; his or hers, it doesn't matter. Another shuddering orgasm, Kerry's education is complete.

"Wow, our best role-play yet," Kerry says a few minutes later, attempting to straighten her clothes in the cramped space of their garden shed, "goodness, I can hardly stand up."

"Lucky you kept your old school uniform and it still fits," replies her husband appreciatively.

"Only just, my bust seems to have grown bigger over the last decade."

"What scene shall we try next?"

"Something more comfortable," pleads Kelly, "I'm not really into unforgiving work surfaces and dust, I want a little luxury for a change."

"Hmm, perhaps a serving girl spanked over her master's four-poster bed -- we could book a night in one of those fancy boutique hotels?"

"Oh, yes please -- I think I've still got my old waitress outfit from when I worked in that tea room during the Uni hols. Little white apron and cap, bit like a maid..."

"Sounds good, I could go down on you, seduce the servant."

"Or I you, service the master, they're not mutually exclusive and I'm getting spanked whatever aren't I?"

"Without a shadow of a doubt."

SERVING DESIRE

Humiliation Bdsm Story

Kelsey reached down and gently cupped my swollen balls, giving them a firm squeeze. She crawled on top of me and smiled, her deep brown eyes looking directly into mine.

"You know our agreement. You get me and in exchange I get to do whatever I want, right?"

I nodded, my cock swelling inside its tight metal cage.

She leaned down, her lips hovering just above mine.

"Beg me to kiss you," she said smiling.

"Please Kelsey, please. I need your lips so much, I am aching for you, please oh God, please kiss me, please," I whined.

"Do you remember the last time I kissed you?" she asked, her warm breath cascading over my lips.

I closed my eyes and nodded.

"And what did I say?" she prodded, with a hint of cruelty in her voice.

I grimaced and bit and breathed in deeply. "That it would be the last time."

She pulled away, sitting up on my chest and letting go of my swollen balls. She winked, "You wouldn't want to make a liar out of me, would you?"

I shook my head. She just sat on me, looking at me, watching. My cheeks turned pink and I closed my eyes.

She chided me, "Now now now. Look at me. I want you to see me."

She slipped her hand into her panties and slid her finger along her pussy before removing it, glistening wet. "You see what this does to me?"

She held her wet finger to my nose. "Sniff it," she commanded.

She giggled as I inhaled. "One more thing you don't get anymore," she said, smiling.

"You stay right here, understand? I am going to go masturbate. You can listen from here. I know you are all locked up," she added, her fingers pulling on the chain on her neck, revealing the small padlock key she wore reminding me of my chastity, "But even so, no touching. Or trying to touch. It only makes it worse when you tug on the cage. You know that right?" I nodded and squirmed as I watched her walk from the room. Her tight t-shirt barely covering the small of her back and her perfect ass framed by her adorable pink cotton panties.

I sat and listened, tortured by the sounds of her orgasms. For the next 20 minutes, she wailed and moaned, cumming more and more each time.

It had been four months since I moved in with Kelsey and this is what my life has become.

It didn't start that way.

Kelsey and I are as different as you can possibly imagine. For starters, there is almost a 30 year age difference. When I met her, she had just turned 19, I was 48.

Kelsey was working as a waitress and I was coming in three or four times a week for breakfast. We struck up a bit of a friendship. She was the most beautiful woman I had ever set eyes on, the perfect girl next door look, with long flowing brown hair and deep brown eyes. Her full lips were impossible to ignore, but also perfect for her look. A cute perky nose, just a few freckles and a body that was like it was molded out of my fantasies. She was athletic, tall and slender. Her smallish breasts gave her a very youthful appearance, but they were certainly enough to make no mistake that she was a woman.

One day when the check arrived, scrawled on the back was a message. "Call me" with her phone number and a heart. When she walked by I stopped her and pointed to the check. "I think you made a mistake, I think this was for someone else," I told her.

She just smiled. "No mistake. Call me."

That evening after work, it took me a dozen times before I could actually make the call.

When I did, I got her voicemail. Fumbling I left a very tense message. "Hi Kelsey, this is um David. You left your number. I mean I think you did. I was just calling. I just. You said call me so I did."

When I put my phone down, my hands were shaking.

20 seconds later my phone rang. I didn't recognize the number.

"Hello?" I asked picking up.

"Hello," the voice came back, unmistakably the voice of Kelsey.

"You called?" she asked.

I cleared my throat. "Um, yes."

"Well? What did you want?" she prodded.

I froze. I didn't know what to say. My hands were trembling again and my heart was pounding.

After what seemed like an eternity, she laughed. "I'm just messing with you. I know I asked you to call me. I bet you are wondering why."

"Now that you mention it, I was," I responded. Before I could finish she interrupted.

"Do you think I am pretty?" she asked.

"Oh God, yes," I responded, perhaps a little too enthusiastically. She laughed.

"I need to know something David. You have to promise to answer me truthfully. Do you promise?"

I agreed.

"Do you think about me when you masturbate?" she asked very plainly.

I stammered and hemmed and hawed, feeling like a deer caught in the headlights.

"You promised to tell me the truth, David. Now tell me. Do you think about me when you masturbate?"

I couldn't speak. After what seemed like an eternity, I closed my eyes and let out the most embarrassing confession of my life.

"Yes."

"I thought so," she said. "See you tomorrow," she added before hanging up.

I didn't sleep a wink, running through my head every possible reason she might ask me that question, what it meant, why I answered the way I did, what else I could have said, and on and on.

Finally, then the clock read 7:00 am, I crawled out of bed, showered and made my way back to the diner, just as I did every Wednesday morning.

I was trembling as my hand touched the door, opened it and I took my usual booth. I sat down and scanned the room, looking for Kelsey.

My heart returned to a somewhat reasonable rate, as I realized she wasn't there. Alice, one of the other waitresses brought my coffee, then my eggs and then the check.

No sign of Kelsey. I was too ashamed to ask.

I left the restaurant crestfallen, hoping I would see her.

As I opened the door and stepped out, I felt a tug on my coat and turned to see a smiling Kelsey. "Miss me?" she asked, her head tilted slightly to the side.

I nodded and smiled weakly back at her. She wrinkled her adorable nose a bit and said "I thought you might have." She started to walk down the street, gently pulling me along by the arm.

"So how are you doing today my little masturbator?" she asked, laughing slightly.

I turned bright red and stopped in my tracks. She

giggled more and gave me a firm tug by the arm.

"Um, fine, I guess," I responded trying to ignore her comment.

"Well that has got to stop. Understand?" she said sternly.

"Thinking about you?" I asked still blushing.

"Oh god no," she laughed, playfully slapping my chest. "The masturbating. I don't mind you thinking about me, fantasizing about me. In fact I want to encourage it."

My head was swimming.

"I need you to promise me David," she said, stopping, turning to me and looking into my eyes.

"I promise," I said, heart pounding again.

"Promise what?" she smiled back at me.

"To stop, you know, what you said," I responded, now blushing more than ever.

She looked at me, a little more directly. "You need to say it. Out loud. Right now."

I nodded, closed my eyes and obeyed. "I promise to stop masturbating, Kelsey." When I opened my eyes, she was grinning ear to ear. "Oh I like it when you say my name, that was hot." She leaned over and pressed her lips to mine, gently and sensually kissing me.

She leaned closer, her lips now just over my ear, whispering in a completely patronizing voice "Such a good little masturbator."

When she pulled away I was looking back at her horrified and ashamed. "Please," I pleaded with her, "pleased don't."

She made the most adorable pouty face and continued in her mocking tone. "When I am convinced you have stopped, I will stop calling you that. Understand?"

I nodded.

She touched my cheek and smiled. "I need to get to class. I'll call you tonight."

I watched her walk away, the sensation of her lips pressed against mine still lingering. My cock was swollen and my first thought was to find some private place where I could relieve the frustration that was building. I thought about my promise and then about her lips.

I went back into the restaurant and slipped into the restroom.

I sat on the toilet and stroked myself until my cock erupted into a wad of toilet paper I was holding. In my mind Kelsey was there, watching, mocking me, calling me names. Her angelic face saying the most humiliating things.

When the phone rang that night, I contemplated not answering. I picked up just before it went to voicemail.

There was a long silence and then she spoke. "Is there something you need to tell me," she asked coldly.
I confessed. "Yes. Yes there is. Just after you left, I went back to the restaurant and did what you asked me not to."

Another long pause. "And what was that?"

"I masturbated," I confessed as a wave of shame came over me.

"And?" she asked. Her tone still sharp.

I froze. "That is it, that is all," I said, feeling genuinely confused.

"No David. That is not all. It isn't even the worst part. You broke a promise. You lied to me. You promised me you would stop masturbating and the first thing you do is run off and jerk off. How am I supposed to trust you?" she lectured.

I felt like a little boy being scolded. "I don't know, I am sorry Kelsey. I won't do it again."

"No, you won't," she said matter of factly. "I am coming over to your place tomorrow at 3:00. We are going to get a few things straight. I have to tell you, I am really on the fence about this. I don't like liars, David."

I tried to explain, but she had already hung up.

I wasn't sure what to do, what to expect or what was happening. All I knew was that my cock was once again rock hard and my balls were swollen. As much as I needed to cum, I decided not to, I tried desperately to focus on something else, anything else.

Another restless night, followed by another breakfast served by Alice. No Kelsey at the diner or at the door.

I cut out of work early, getting home at 2:00, taking a shower and picking out something to wear that would make me feel good. The place was clean and I had a bottle of wine in the fridge.

At exactly 3:00 there was a knock at the door.

When I opened it, Kelsey was standing there, looking somewhat displeased. She had a long coat on and carried a large Coach bag. She pointed to the chair and directed me. "Sit," was all she said.

She took over her coat, revealing a crisp white blouse and a black pencil skirt. She looked almost like an old- style school marm, but also incredibly sexy.

"We have a few things to get straight," she told me.

"I want to make a deal with you. It should be obvious by now that I am looking for a sexual relationship and that I am considering you as the person to do that with. You also can see that you are older than I am. I am guessing 25 maybe 30 years. I get off on controlling older men. The rules are simple. I get to do whatever I want to you. That is going to include humiliating you and keeping you desperate and sexually frustrated.

That is my fetish. What you get out of it is being with me. Being near me, close to me, wanting me and needing me. I am going to be your addiction. I won't be good for you, but you won't be able to help yourself."

She looked down at me. "Do you understand what I am telling you?" I nodded.

"Then say it."

"I understand what you are telling me, Kelsey."

She smiled. "To make this work, you need to be completely honest with me about everything. No secrets. When I ask a question, you won't hesitate or think about it. You will tell me, right?"

I nodded. She looked at me, clearly letting me know I was testing her patience.

"I will tell you Kelsey."

"Now as much as I adore honesty, you should know that you won't get that from me. I am going to lie to you, trick you, and generally fuck with your head. That is what you are signing up for with me. Sometimes I will use honesty to hurt you. Sometimes I will lie to you just for my own amusement."

"That doesn't seem fair," I interjected.

"It's not David. But it is the price for being with me. If you don't accept these terms I will understand. I know this is an unusual arrangement. If you don't agree to everything, we can just walk away. But once you agree to my terms, that is it. There is no escape or negotiation."

She opened her bag and placed a written document on the table. Next to it was a small black bag.

"When I come back tomorrow, I will expect two things. The first is your signature on that contract, which spells out the terms of our relationship. The second is a chastity cage for your cock. There is a lock but no key.

Once it is on, I will be the only person able to unlock it."

Kelsey smiled and came over to where was sitting raising her skirt, revealing herself completely to me. No panties, just her gorgeous pussy. She kneeled down and started to stroke my cock through my pants. Soon she was lowering the zipper and sliding my cock out, continuing to stroke it.

She took my hand and led me to the middle of the room and placed me on my back, lowering herself over me, her wet pussy covering my face.

"Masturbate for me," she commanded. I squirmed under her pussy and ass, struggling to breathe as I started to stroke myself.

"I can't wait to lock up your tiny little dick, loser," she hissed. "Smell me, masturbator, lick my wet stinky pussy. Show me how fucking pathetic you are."

The more she talked the wetter I could feel her getting.

"That isn't even a cock, it is so fucking small. You are never getting that thing inside me. I wouldn't even be able to feel it," she continued laughing now.

"Don't you care cum," she commanded.

Soon I could feel her starting to shake, pressing down hard so I couldn't breathe at all. I squirmed and struggled as she yanked my hand away from my cock and started slapping my cock. One hand grabbed my balls, squeezing them cruelly.

I screamed into her as she began to cum, her hand now slapping my cock really hard, the stinging becoming almost unbearable.
Just when I was about to pass out from lack of air, she rolled off me, collapsing into her own state of bliss. Her hand slid down between her legs, as she gently touched herself, giving herself another round of more subdued orgasms.

Her fingers traced over my cheeks, coated in her juices.

"Don't wash your face until I see you again."

"I won't wash my face until I see you again Kelsey," I

said. My response bringing a smile to her face.

I looked down at my bright red cock, still hard but too sensitive to touch.

"You won't be able to rub that for a while, now will you?" she giggled.

I blushed more.

She gathered herself and her things and within a few minutes, she was back to her normal appearance, save for a radiant glow that seemed to come from every part of her.

"Tomorrow at 7:00, I will be back. You have a lot to think about masturbator."

When the door shut behind her, I burst into tears, not ever sure why. That night, I tried to masturbate several times, but the pain in my cock was too much. My thoughts would be me hard, but the skin was too tender to touch, creating an intense frustration.

I slept naked, on my back with no covers. My rock hard cock, twitching and aching for relief I couldn't provide.

Against all better judgement, I picked up the phone and called Kelsey. I didn't even know what I was going to say. When her groggy voice answered the words just came out. "Kelsey, I need you."

"I know," she said and hung up.

By morning, the swelling in my cock had subsided enough to allow me to get dressed, though the pain would be a constant reminder of Kelsey throughout the day.

When I got home, I spent the next two hours reading through the contract. I debated with myself back and forth. She was right about two things: this wasn't good for me and I desperately needed it.
Finally, when I was at peace with myself and fully understood what I was signing up for I took the pen and signed my name, just about the line that she would sign below.

I opened the black bag and found four metal pieces. It took a few minutes to figure out the design, but eventually I did. I placed the ring behind my balls, closing it and securing it with a small pin. Next came the cage itself, which was only 2" long, but fit my cock perfectly when it was soft, filling every bit of the cage, but still comfortable. Finally, I picked up the small silver lock. It was unlike any I had seen before. It had a very unconventional key slot and was much lighter than I thought it would be. I sat for 15 minutes before I steeled up my courage to snap the lock shut.

The moment I did, my sore cock began to swell in its cage. At first there was discomfort and then after trying to adjust it, I realized it was starting to be painful. As my cock pressed into the cage and my skin pressed through the openings, it grew more and more painful. I tugged and yanked trying to free myself, to no avail. I ran to the freezer and started to pack my cock in ice,

which helped to numb it but not with the swelling. I tried thinking unsexy thoughts, but my mind kept returning to the thought of Kelsey standing there watching and laughing, pointing at me and giggling about the pain my own erection was causing me.

The thought was making things worse.

Finally, after almost an hour, my cock had begun to return to its smaller incarnation, relieving most of the pressure. At 7:00 there was a knock on the door.

Looking stunning, Kelsey stood before me. She took one look at my face and smiled.

She brushed past me and over the the table, where she held up the black bag that had held the device. She turned up upside down and shook it.

"Good boy," she said, smiling.

"Now, about this," she said, tapping her finger on the contract. "I see you have signed."

I nodded. "Yes Kelsey. I have signed."

"But I haven't," she said. It was something I hadn't considered.

"That device you have on is made of titanium. You can't cut it. You can't break it. The lock too. It is on until I decide to remove it. The lock is impossible to pick."

She picked up the contract and looked over it.

"This contract is the only thing stopping me from walking out that door forever, leaving you in permanent chastity with me as a memory. One you won't even be able to masturbate anymore."

She came closer.

"Most guys would be kicking and screaming right now, threatening me, demanding to be released. But not you. All you are thinking is how can I get her to sign that contract? Terrified I might leave. You know I am going to be a nightmare for you, but you are willing to endure that just so I don't leave, aren't you. A deep, sick part of

you actually enjoys it. Needs it. Wants to beg for it."

I looked into her eyes and nodded. "I need you

Kelsey." "I know" she said.

I have no idea what came over me, but at that moment, I kneeled down and pressed my lips down to her shoes and kissed them. "Please Kelsey, please sign the contract and make my life a nightmare. You can do anything you want to me Kelsey, just let me be near you. Please."

I felt her press the paper to my back and sign her name. "I'm sorry," she said. It would be the last time she would ever apologize to me.

MASTER HAREM

Master and Slave Bdsm Story

I lay back on a big relaxing soft pile of thick luxurious Arabic pillows, overstuffed and with embroidered velvet covers, ornate golden tassels on the corners. There were many more such big rich pillows all over the floor of the room, and even some big piles of them piled up to the low eight-foot ceiling. The ceiling had luxurious deep-shag Arabic rugs hanging from it, and other rich-colored soft deep rugs covered the free space on the floors and walls, giving the whole room an enclosed, relaxing, nest-like feeling. The room was mostly in a cool shade, with bright light and a soft warm breeze coming from a massive open window that looked out on a broad wide blindingly bright desert valley far below. It was a breathtaking view that stretched out for miles.

I sank down deeper into the pile of pillows, waves of pleasure and relaxation surging through my body, pure heaven emanating in thick waves from between my legs. I brought my eyes back from the window, looking off at the bright far away desert hills, and looked down to between my open thighs. Through half-closed eyes, I saw Violet's pretty, innocent, slightly rounded young face entranced in a bliss of her own, as she worshipped my cock with her mouth. She was good at it, too, with thick, full-mouthed slurping, perfectly emulating fucking a tight vagina with the rhythm of her suctioned mouth, her tongue massaging the underside of my crown in a thick massaging motion as my shaft rocked in and out between her lipsticked girl-lips. If she felt my pleasure surge up too high, too close to reaching the peak of pleasure and flooding her little mouth with my sticky hungry seed, she did as exactly she had been trained : to extend the experience, she would alternate with some slower, lighter licking up and down the length of my shaft, until my pleasure subsided back down away from the edge.

I felt relaxing rich tingles from my ballsack and perineum, where Violet was gently using her long, tapered nails and soft finger pads to smoothly massage and lightly scratch me. Every once in a while, she would slide her soft girlish lipsticked lips and tongue down the entire front line of the shaft of my cock, and thickly, lovingly, and attentively lick my scrotum and along my perineum. She would attentively use her clean fresh young lips and tongue to debase herself by licking circles around the nasty dirty ring of my anus, before traveling back up, smoothly and lovingly sucking in my each testicle in turn, before returning to worshipping my cock. My world got a little watery as the pleasure built higher and higher, looking down to see her radiant angelic feminine face framed and locked in place by my muscular hairy man's legs as I clenched them against her. Heat rose up the front of my body as I watched the thick shaft of my cock disappearing into and reappearing out of her pretty young over-lipsticked mouth, violating her pretty young innocence, as she left little caked lipstick rings smudged up and down its length as she bobbed her soft mouth up and down.

I gazed on her pretty young eyes caked up with thick slutty eyeliner, heavy mascara on showgirl-length false eyelashes, and heavy eyeshadow in a color that complimented her large hazel eyes. Her jet-black lustrous long hair was pulled back from her smooth teenage olive-toned face by a girlish pink hair bow. I especially enjoyed letting my eyes travel along her legs kicked out to the side, her red-painted toenails poking out of five-inch spike stripper spike-heeled pumps, held on to her delicate ankle by a tiny little buckle, delicate filmy shiny opaque grey stockings encasing her smooth young legs, with exposed naked soft girl leg flesh above the band at the top of the silky stockings. Her free hand was buried underneath her short pleated black skirt, vigorously pumping. It was obvious that she was doing just as she had been trained, furiously frigging her clit to orgasmic pleasure of her own. I knew, however, that, given how she had also been trained, she probably would have felt a full, even orgasmic pleasure just from giving her full heart's devotion to fucking her face on my cock ...

Finally, I wanted it for real. I softly said "now", and the obedient, eager-to-please Violet fucked her mouth onto my dick double time. Her inner cheeks tightened up the suction around my thick shaft, her head bobbed up and down at a rapid pace, tongue swirling along the underside of my corona. A thick wave of pleasure overtook me, and the world blanked out, and I met God for just a second. I came to, feeling the muscles in my groin rhythmically contracting, as I spurted thick spurts of jism into the adoring mouth of the young girl. She wrapped her mouth around my pulsating rod as if I was shooting liquid diamonds, making sure to capture every last drop. As the my spurting died down, Violet settled her curvy delicate skirted form between my legs, softly holding them apart with her long, radiantly red fingernails, and, lightly moaning and trembling herself, lightly, delicately, lovingly slowly licked up and down along the underside of my shaft to extend my orgasmic sensation. She did so with care, because she had my fresh hot load of sticky semen within her soft mouth.

In a little bit, Violet reached over, and with a well-practiced motion, used her long-nailed feminine hand to ring a small brass bell that had been sitting next to her. With this, a door to our left softly opened, and in walked another stunningly, radiantly beautiful young Arab girl, tottering precariously on four inch cork platform wedge heels that gave her an exaggeratedly feminine hip roll and a look of constantly being about to topple over in. She was dressed similarly to Violet : shimmery gossamer grey opaque thigh high stockings encasing the soft curves of her girlish calves and legs (with the grey stretched nylon just translucent enough to reveal the bright red toenails that extended beyond the straps of her towering platform wedges), a thin vulnerable sliver of soft female thigh flesh between the tops of the stockings and a brief pleated black skirt that barely covered her feminine charms and that swayed beguilingly around her hips as she walked. Around her midsection was a tight dull-black leather corset that constrained her into an exaggerated hourglass figure, visibly restrained her from full breathing, and pushed up and supported the underside her unnaturally massive outsized breasts. Her translucent filmy white long-sleeve blouse covered the huge nurturing breasts, but was sheer enough that I could see tiny nipple clamps affixed to each nipple. I knew that the girl had worn nipple clamps enough times that the sharp pain no longer distracting her from what she was doing, and instead just washed through her as she walked, bringing a certain submissive pleasure-intensity to her. And like Violet, she wore a leather collar with a silver slave ring around her neck, and angelic young face with a cute upturned nose and a sweet friendly smile, slathered in heavy slutty makeup, thick mascara on her long dark eyelashes that looked so arousing when she batted her eyes. Her long silky black hair constrained in two girlish pony tails in the back and, in the front, pulled back from her pretty young face by a pink hair bow. She also had her long fingernails painted a beautifully bright red fuck-me color.

Hailey, this girl who had just entered, tottered in subserviently, nervously, with her head slightly bowed, seemingly approval-seeking and excited in my presence. When she got to the pile of pillows upon which I reclined, with Violet between my legs, Hailey did a full-prostration deep bow before me, long black-haired pony tails draping down over her cute pink hair ribbon as she bowed. She then smiled nervously, and cuddled up to Violet. Hailey's brief black skirt rose up around her thighs and up to her left hip as she got seated, revealing at the cleft where her soft fertile inner thighs met, her most private treasure, sheer nylon pink panties barely covering the two shaved bald lips of her soft pubic mound. She smiled shyly as she noticed me looking at her barely pantied fertile young vagina, seemingly pleased, doing nothing to pull down her obscenely angled skirt. I could see slight spots of damp moisture set against the pink nylon mesh.

Violet looked at Hailey and smiled, and Hailey dropped her pretty face in a subordinate position below Violet's.

Violet slowly opened her lipsticked mouth, and a thick ropey strand of my baby-making juice and Violet's mouth juices twisted down from Violet's pretty lipsticked mouth into Hailey's. The scene was as dirty as it was hot, one sweet pretty feminine creature impregnating the mouth of a compliant other sweet pretty feminine creature with the animal juice from my balls. Both girls seemed to relish swallowing the load of jizz in their months, and looked pleased and satisfied afterwards.

I knew that Hailey had been waiting outside the door for the honor of sharing in some of my seed. The girls of the house vied amongst themselves to consume my load, so much so that rules about sharing had had to be set up. I also knew that Hailey was Violet's "Almarwuws" in the house pecking order, or subordinate, a newer girl to the house. This meant that Hailey would be the one to receive from Violet, and, in general, to obey her, and, unless I gave instructions otherwise, to sexually submit to her, should the situation arise. In the case of these two girls, this dominance order was natural, given Violet's more outgoing nature. Sometimes, the rule took more enforcing - which could be lots of fun, if we wanted it to be.

I stroked both of the sweet girl's soft heads of hair, as they draped themselves against my legs, huge soft baby-feeding milk-jug breasts pressed flat on my upper calves, the leather of their tight corsets smooth against my lower calves, impossibly tall spike heels off to one side on the floor and dauntingly tall cork wedges off to the other. The kittens lay there, soft and warm, back- to-back, making high pitched cooing, mewing, cuddling against me lovingly, slowly grinding their short skirted asses against each other lasciviously. As their ass cheeks rubbed, the black pleats of their tiny skirts rose, revealing the smooth impossibly firm globes of their smooth teenage ass cheeks, split only by the thin, almost translucent pink strip of whoreish thong panty fabric gripping their ass cracks.

After a few minutes, my muscular male arms lifted both of them up and off of me, and I got up to my feet. As I left, still in an erotic haze, the girls collapsed into the piles of pillows, an erotically charged tangle of limbs, smooth stockinged leg wrapped entangled around smooth stockinged leg, huge constrained breasts pressed up against the same, lipsticked mouth exploring lipsticked mouth, red fingernailed hands exploring and caressing, Hailey submissively giving in to the more dominant Violet's rough advances. They briefly stopped to look up at me adoringly as I walked to the door, and then continued with their lesbian animal rutting, sheer pink pantied soaking wet young pubic mound grinding rhythmically and enthusiastically against sheer pink pantied soaking wet young pubic mound.

PLAY THING

Domination Bdsm Story

It all started quite innocently. Jane and I had been dating for nearly a year and our relationship had hit a low point. Just when I thought it was over she suggested we try something different. Sexually different. I wasn't entirely sure about the look in her eye or her eagerness but she had me at "sexually different".

She invited me over for a special dinner one evening insisting that we get dressed up for it. She looked absolutely stunning in a body clinging dress that was very nearly sheer and left very little to the imagination and my imagination was telling me she was naked beneath it. The dinner was exceptional with several courses of delicious creations, plenty of wine and a happy pleasant banter between us. I was sated and euphoric when Jane announced that there was still dessert to be served. I groaned, teasingly, moaning about being too full but willing to try to sample anything she had created.

Jane smiled coyly at me from across the table. With a mischievous arching of her eyebrows she slowly slipped from view. At first I thought it was my imagination but I finally realized that she was sliding out of her chair and onto the floor. It took my wine addled brain a moment to mesh special dessert with Jane's behavior. My confusion soon vanished when to my pleasant surprise Jane's fingers began caressing my knees from beneath the table.

Jane soon had me panting with anticipation as she caressed my thighs working her way towards my swelling groin. She had always been able to drive me to distraction sexually and her performance underneath the table was no exception. Slowly, deliberately Jane exposed my now throbbing member as I fought to control my breathing. I lost track of time as Jane's warm soft hands worked their magic over my swollen cock before gasping audibly when her hot mouth enveloped the head.

Jane's mouth on my erection pulled my butt off the seat of the chair giving her more access to my cock. I had to grip the chair to steady myself as Jane's hot mouth and soft fingers went to town on my manhood. Her enthusiasm and talents were soon too much for me. As she felt my orgasm building Jane changed tactics, slowing down, deliberately squeezing my balls slightly to distract me. Her hot moist mouth left my cock to the cooler night air as her face slipped between my thighs. One hand continued to squeeze gently, then harder, then gently on my balls while the other slowly, purposefully stroked my spit slick erection.

Kissing my thighs and nuzzling with her nose Jane gently forced me to spread my legs further for her. With my buttocks hanging off the chair seat and Jane's hands holding my cock and balls I was entirely at her mercy. Jane used her tongue to aggressively assault the sensitive area beneath my balls. Forcing her face between my thighs Jane playfully nipped me there with her sharp teeth. When I yelped in surprise and shifted away from the tingling pain her hand closed meaningfully over my balls holding me still. While her other hand continued to slowly stroke my throbbing pole Jane squeezed my balls and nipped me again. This time instead of yelping I moaned. Jane's tongue flicked between my legs, her grip pumped my balls while her hand stroked my cock, my head swirled, my entire body tingled with sexual tension.

Jane's teeth were nipping playfully at my buttocks making me flinch and twitch, her tongue caressed it's way between my ass cheeks. I gasped wildly disbelieving that she would even dare to before my next gasp turned into a soundless scream of pleasure as simultaneously Jane's tongue entered my anus while her fingers gripped my balls pulling my body towards her and her tongue deeper inside me. Despite the discomfort emanating from my balls my body twitched and lurched with Jane's tongue swirling about and in my anus. My body was racing towards sensation overload when my my cock erupted in Jane's hand. I howled with the intense mixture of pleasure and pain as my body convulsed uncontrollably within Jane's grip.

As my body trembled and pulsed and lurched with the most explosive orgasm I had ever experienced Jane's tongue exited my ass. With a playful nip that I barely noticed she pulled her face from between my thighs. Watching my bodies reactions with a amused smile Jane kissed my balls before releasing them. Her hand still gently stroked my cum slick and very sensitive cock. My breathes came in long gasping swallows as my body continued to twitch and quiver. My face was tingling and my brain was numb as Jane's hand pulled me mewing with distress from the chair by my still erect manhood.

When I plopped unceremoniously onto the floor before her Jane smiled knowingly, beaming with pleasure at my sex devastated state. Her hand held me by my cock while her thumb caressed the sensitive head. Jane assessed me intensely, powerfully. Licking her lips lasciviously her grip tightened drawing a long quivering gasp from my distraught body. Without relinquishing her grip Jane's other hand busily pulled at my clothes eventually stripping me naked from the waist down. She had me panting spellbound as the fingers of her free hand slipped beneath the hem of her dress.

Holding my gaze I witnessed the slight fluttering of her eyes as I imagined her fingers finding her pussy. Jane's chest heaved stretching the sheer material over her bra-less breasts. Her nipples protruded rock hard while her head lolled back exposing the length of her neck. I watched transfixed as her lips parted and she gasped with a giggling pleasure. Had she just had a mini orgasm I wondered.

Jane's hand never left my erection, panting slightly herself Jane's other hand was suddenly there between us. Even in the dull light under the table I could see the that it was slick with secretions. Her smile turned mischievous as she held her fingers out for me to see. Slowly she edged her body up mine bringing her fingers closer to my face holding them beneath my nose so that I could smell her excitement. Breathing in deeply I closed my eyes to enhance the experience of her scent. When I licked my lips Jane giggled again then traced my lips with her now sticky fingers. The sensation of her finger tips on my lips was electric. Sighing with need I pulled at them with my lips. Jane giggled again feeding me her scent tainted fingers as her body continued to edge up over mine.

The hem of Jane's clinging dress had risen high on her thighs and I could feel the heat of her womanhood on my bare flesh. Opening my eyes I stared wonderingly into hers as the stretched hem of her dress made contact with her hand still stroking my rock hard cock. Jane leaned towards me, her slick fingers held my face still. Her tongue darted out seductively to lick her parted lips before her hot mouth covered mine. Jane kissed me deeply, passionately, I moaned wantonly in response. At some point she had managed to pull her dress up further on her body. With our mouths locked passionately together Jane pressed her body onto mine gurgling with a surge of fervor when our sex met. I was rock hard in her grasp and I moaned uncontrollably as Jane held me firmly rocking her hips to pump her pussy over the head of my cock.

Her fingers hadn't lied, Jane was sopping wet with her excitement. The warm wet of her cunt was soon coating her hand and my cock. Jane used my cock head relentlessly to massage her slick clit. Her hand had slipped behind my head pulling my face into hers as she kissed me with a growing ferocity. We were both panting and moaning in heat when Jane's clutching fingers directed my cock to the opening of her sopping cunt and her rocking hips plunged down impaling her on my manhood. Jane threw back her head howling with passion. I could only gasp for breath as her deliciously warm pussy clutched spasmodically at my cock and she pressed herself onto me. With my mouth gaping open Jane thrust her pussy juice soaked fingers into it.

Our eyes locked onto each others. Jane's fingers ripped at my hair pulling head back. Her other hand roughly spread her juices over my face while she began to slowly pump her pussy up and down on my cock. Jane fucked me. Jane fucked me with determination. Jane stared right through me as she used my cock for her pleasure. I watched spellbound ignoring the harshness of her hands as her assault on my body intensified. Jane's audible groans rose every time her pumping hips impaled her pussy on my cock. Soon she was pile driving herself onto me with abandon.

As suddenly as her assault had intensified it ended. Jane froze with my cock deep inside her. Holding her breath in a silent scream her fingers gripped my head and face painfully. Slowly her head began to rock back and forth, then her hips. Jane's pussy clenched over my cock and with a gasp of pain I erupted deep inside her. Distracted by her own intense sexual passions Jane didn't seem to notice nor care. With her hips still rotating slightly, gently Jane let the weight of her body press me back and into the floor. Behind us my chair crashed to the floor and though Jane flinched at the noise her body continued to rest onto mine.

Jane's breath came in long shuddering gasps into my neck and her body trembled slightly as I held her close. Just when I thought she had fallen asleep she began to nuzzle my neck her lips pecking at my flesh. My cock had finally deflated and when it slipped wetly from Jane's hot steamy cunt she sighed then bit me. I gasped at the unexpectedness but before I could utter a complaint Jane pressed her hands onto my shoulders to push herself upright astride my groin. Staring down at me dully Jane's fingers slipped into the collar of my shirt. Clutching fists full of material she wrenched her arms apart sending a shower of buttons clattering across the floor. Manically she seethed as she wrenched a second time to expose my bare chest. I could only behold her in stunned silence.

Jane's chest heaved with the frenzy of her efforts. Jane slowly began to crawl up my prone body. Her legs pressed into my bare sides as she knelt over. Staring deeply into my eyes Jane lifted first one knee and then the other pinning my shoulders to the floor beneath her. Holding me captivated Jane ran fingers seductively, lasciviously up and down her bare thighs pushing the hem of her dress higher with each lingering stroke exposing more and more of her creamy white thighs. I knew what was coming. Laying there watching mesmerized as this sexual beauty exposed herself I realized the aching from my groin was my painfully engorging cock. Returning Jane's intense stare I gaped at the wonder of her as her pink puffy pussy slipped into view.

Astounded it took me a moment to realize that Jane

had shaved her pussy hair. While I stared marveling at the difference it made Jane's thighs spread and her amazing womanhood lowered over my face. Jane held herself just above my mouth enveloping my senses in the mixture of my own cum and her sexual funk. Ever so slowly she started to rock her hips back and forth lightly brushing her pussy over my lips and nose. As I drank in the scent of sex Jane pressed lower. Soon her slick cunt lips parted as they passed over my nose. I took a long shuddering breath filled with the scent of her and heard Jane gurgle with appreciation above me.

Jane stopped with her pussy lips spread over the tip of my nose. She was all I could smell, all I could taste. My chest heaved as I began to drown on the heady aroma of her. Jane used my nose to teasingly caress her pussy lips with. Her wetness was soon coating her thighs and my face. Suddenly Jane sank onto my face. She allowed the weight of her body to spread her steamy moist cunt over me. Straddling my face Jane began to grind herself onto my mouth and nose. When my lungs began to burn with need I struggled to throw her off. I was beginning to realize it was useless and just as I felt I would pass out Jane raised herself to allow me a few gasping cummy cunt scented breathes before sinking down over me again. Her hand was wrenching at my hair as she ground her mound onto my face.

Jane's frantic rocking hips humped my nose and chin. I could hear her wailing as she rode my face. Then Jane's world exploded in orgasmic pleasure. Her cunt gushed a mixture of our juices. As she bucked violently I was allowed short cum filled gasps of breath. I had never witnessed an orgasm like Jane's. As it dissipated I was terrified when Jane's pussy sank wetly back over my mouth and nose. I whimpered and struggled feebly beneath Jane as she gasped and twitched spasmodically on my face. I was left to gasp like a fish out of water when finally spent Jane eventually slumped to the floor releasing my face from her pussy.

Panting I listened to Jane moaning lightly with pleasure beside me. Licking my lips I tasted the sticky goo coating them and raised myself on an elbow. I reached over to gently stroke Jane's still slightly trembling body. Murmuring nonsense she rolled into me to snuggle in post orgasmic euphoria. Our hands casually caressed each other until Jane's exploring fingers discovered my erect member. Giggling with delight her fingers closed over my cock possessively.

"More dessert," she whispered seductively in my ear. I whimpered as her hand began to squeeze and pump my sex sensitive cock but didn't even think to stop her.

PERFECT MISTRESS

Mistress And Slave Bdsm Story

Matt sat on the edge of the bed looking down at the steel tube which encased his cock. He'd waited so long for this moment, but still he was tremendously nervous. As he looked down he caught sight of his face, reflected in the highly polished surface of the chastity device. Could he really go through with this? He steeled himself and pushed the small padlock through the locking holes and snapped it shut. His breathing was heavy as he dressed quickly, determined to get this part over with quickly before he backed out of it once again.

He walked down the stairs, the two small keys pressed firmly into his palm. About half way down the stairs he panicked. What was he doing? What was he thinking? What would she think? He paused on the stairs, his mind in turmoil as he debated whether to retreat back upstairs, but now it was too late, she was calling him.

"Matt!"

He froze like a deer in headlights, squeezing the keys tighter and tighter until they left an imprint in his palm.

"Matt!"

Matt slowly took the last few steps to the bottom of the stairs to see his gorgeous wife Suzanne standing there holding out a jar.

"Can you open this for me please?"

Matt looked at her stupidly. They had been married for six years now, but he still found her absolutely stunning and couldn't believe he had been so lucky as to marry a woman like her.

"Oh, yes, of course."

He reached out to take the jar and then realised that he was still holding the keys to his chastity device. He quickly stuffed them into his pocket and opened the jar with relative ease. Suzanne kissed him on the cheek and took the jar back before returning to the kitchen.

Matt watched her walk through the kitchen door and stood in the middle of the lounge feeling slightly foolish. He noticed he was trembling slightly, but worked up the courage to follow her into the kitchen.

He surveyed the worksurfaces and quickly realised that she was in the middle of cooking something.

"Are you busy?" he asked.

"Well yes, a little," she said.

"Oh, okay...it doesn't matter."

He turned to leave, but Suzanne sensed something was up and called him back.

"I know that look," she said mischievously. "What have you done?"

Matt couldn't help but smile to himself, he was prone to nervous laughter at the best of times.

"Umm, can I talk to you for a moment, in here?"

"Sure," she said, looking a little apprehensive as she followed him into the lounge.

"Sit down... please," said

Matt.

Suzanne sat on the sofa and Matt sat down next to

her. "I.   I have something to give you."

He fished in his pocket and retrieved the small key ring and two keys, he held them out to his wife saying "I. ....I would like you to have these."

Suzanne looked at the two small keys hanging from her husband's fingers. She instantly knew what they were for, but she was still more than a little surprised. She continued to stare at them as Matt twitched nervously next to her.

"Are they what I think they are?" she asked softly.

"Y...yes," he stammered.

She looked at him, a mixture of emotions bubbling over inside.

"Are you sure you want to do this?"

He paused for a moment, concentrating his

thoughts. "Yes... I'm sure."

The silence hung heavily in the air as they looked at each other, Suzanne still not making any move for the keys.

"And you understand what this

means?" "Yes..."

Suzanne arched an eyebrow slightly and Matt hastily corrected himself.

"Yes, Mistress."

Suzanne reached out and held her upturned palm under the keys. Matt let go and the two keys clinked together as they fell into her hand.

"Thank you," she said and leaned over to kiss him.

As they broke they kiss, Suzanne said two words; "Show me."

Matt understood immediately and stood up. He undid his button and pushed his trousers and boxers down in one movement, revealing the highly polished metal chastity device that encased his cock. Suzanne gasped as she saw the curved tube for the first time. She had only seen plastic chastity devices before, cheap-looking horrible things, but this was quite different. She reached out and traced her finger along the length of the tube and then moved down to softly massage Matt's balls, causing his cock to swell inside the tube.

"Mmmmm," purred Suzanne. "Is it comfortable?"

"Yes... I've worn it on and off for a month... I wanted to make sure that it was okay before

I gave you the keys."

"I see... what's the longest you've had it

on?" "About three days."

"And it was okay?"

"It chaffed a little, but a little cream sorted it."

Suzanne smiled and bent her head closer to her husband's groin. He felt her breath on his balls and then her tongue flicking against them, coating them with her saliva. Matt's cock was quickly as hard as it could get inside the tight tube and he was soon groaning as she sucked his balls into her mouth, knowing full well what she was doing to him.

Matt looked down and saw that Suzanne had hitched up her thin red summer dress and was rubbing her pussy as she tormented him. The sight of his beautiful wife giving herself pleasure at the very moment that he had surrendered his own to her was almost too much for him. Abruptly Suzanne let go of him and leaned back on the sofa, spreading her legs and exposing her soaking wet knickers to him. Matt was on his knees in seconds, while Suzanne lay back further and lifted herself up so that he could peel away the wet cotton.

Matt tossed the damp panties to one side and then moved closer, drinking in the sight of his wife's delicious pussy. He breathed deeply, inhaling her luscious scent and then bent closer, gently kissing the small patch of neatly trimmed hair above her slit.

Then, overcome with need he buried his face in her delicious pussy, expertly teasing her lips with his own, pulling on them gently while pressing his hand down softly on her mound. Suzanne was soon grinding her aching cunt against him, moving herself so that her clit was in line with her husband's mouth. Matt took the hint and gently started to use his tongue to stimulate the hood of her sensitive bud and then, almost before he had started, Suzanne's body spasmed wildly, taking him completely by surprise as she shuddered through a massive orgasm. Matt kept licking her, savouring every drop of her beautiful juice until Suzanne pushed his head away and begged him to stop. Matt looked up in total shock, he had never seen his wife cum so fast in his life!

"Wow," breathed Suzanne, smiling down at him. "That was... amazing!"

Matt didn't know what to say, his eyes were irresistibly drawn back between her beautiful smooth legs to her gorgeous, wet, pussy and he couldn't resist leaning forward and gently mopping up her juices with his tongue, carefully avoiding her over-sensitive clit. Matt adored the taste of his wife's pussy and Suzanne was used to having him clean up her juices, his too for that matter... although given this latest turn of events it occurred to her that he might not be doing that again for a little while...

After a short while Suzanne recovered and sat up, while Matt remained kneeling in front of her. She bent down and pushed the key into the small padlock and turned it until she heard a small click. Suzanne twisted the padlock open and slowly slid the curved metal bar out of the rings in the top of the chastity device. She sat up and put the padlock to one side and then bent down to remove the metal tube from Matt's cock. The tube slid off fairly easily and within seconds Matt's cock was pointing upwards and rock hard.

"Now," said Suzanne. "Do you remember what I said to you when you asked me if I would be your keyholder?"

"Yes Mistress, you said that if I really wanted to wear a chastity device...that I would have to follow your rules to the letter."

"And what were those rules slave?"

"I must give you total control of my cock... I must give you all the keys to the padlock... I must accept that you will only unlock me when you wish to play with my cock... I must accept that being unlocked does not necessarily mean that I will get to cum or even that you will touch me..."

"Go on."

"I must always be ready to pleasure you Mistress...."

"And?"

"If I am allowed to cum... I must lick it up from wherever it lands, Mistress."

"Very good slave, although I think you have forgotten one..."

Matt looked quizickally at his wife and Mistress.

"You must accept that there may be long periods when you are not allowed to cum, and you must NEVER cum without permission."

"Yes Mistress, sorry Mistress."

"And you accept all these rules

slave?" "Yes Mistress."

"Good. Well it looks like it needs some attention, so why don't you stroke it for me?"

"Yes Mistress, thank you Mistress..."

Matt reached down and curled his hand around his

rock hard length, he slowly began to jerk his meat as his eyes were irresistibly drawn to the wet slippery flesh between his Mistress's thighs. Suzanne leaned back and opened her legs to give him a better view of the beautiful slit he craved so much, her fingers sliding either side and squeezing her pink lips together before peeling them apart to show him just what he was giving up for her.

"Oh slave, what have you done... once you're locked up only I will get to decide when your cock is released and only I will decide if it is to be allowed inside my beautiful pussy... and that might not be very often at all. Can you live with that slave, or would you rather just throw in the towel now and go back to a normal life."

Matt looked at her, the tiniest hint of doubt lingering in his eyes.

"I only want what you want Mistress".

Suzanne smiled as she watched his hand pumping his cock a little harder now.

"Don't you cum without permission," she warned.

"No Mistress," replied Matt breathlessly as he stared longingly at Suzanne's dripping wet cunt.

"If you cum without my permission your first stint in the tube will be one you'll never forget!"

Suzanne lifted up her foot and pressed the instep against Matt's balls.

"These are mine too," she said sharply, before softly kicking his balls.

"Yes Mistress," agreed Matt as his cock grew harder still.

"Right, I want to see you edge."

Matt looked up into her eyes and breathed heavily as his hand moved faster on his cock.

"Don't you dare cum without permission," she reminded him tersely.

Matt pumped his cock hard until he felt the tell-tale signs of approaching orgasm.

"I'm there Mistress," he gasped, loosening his grip on his straining cock.

Suzanne bent down and batted his hands away, before very softly stroking his throbbing, aching, desperate cock a few times, only stopping when she saw a clear drop of fluid appear at the tip of his cock. Suzanne dragged her finger across the tip of his cock, collecting the drop of pre-cum carefully and then watching intently as he obediently licked her finger clean.

"You're going to be tasting that a lot," she smirked. "A lot more than you're going to be tasting your cum, that's for sure."

Matt gasped as his cock throbbed madly, threatening to erupt even without the benefit of direct stimulation. Suzanne looked down at his stalk pulsing madly and closed her legs.

"I think that's enough for today, in future I will want at least two or three edges, but I think you are a little too excited today, and I don't want any accidents."

"No Mistress, thank you Mistress."

Suzanne leaned forward as if to kiss him but instead pressed her mouth close to his ear and whispered, "Wouldn't you just love to grab it, pump it and spray your cum all over my beautiful feet slave?"

"Oh God yes Mistress..."

"Even though you know that you would have to lick up and swallow every single drop of your cum?"

"Yes Mistress, please..."

Suzanne chuckled to herself softly.

"No slave, not today...not today."